This Boxer Books paperback belongs to

. . . .

WITHDRAWN

For OGF, with love
Bernette Ford

For Boxer Books
Sam Williams

First published in Great Britain in 2006
by Boxer Books Limited.
www.boxerbooks.com

ISBN 1-905417-00-4

5 7 9 10 8 6 4

Printed in China

NAPPY DUCK
and
POTTY PIGGY

Bernette Ford and Sam Williams

Boxer Books

Ducky knocks on Piggy's door.

No-one answers.

"Come out, Piggy," she calls.

"Come out and play with me."

Piggy is busy.

"I can't come out now," he calls.

"I am sitting on the potty!"

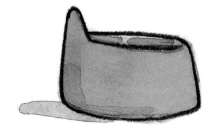

Ducky goes inside.

She goes into Piggy's room.

She plays with Piggy's toys.

She reads Piggy's books.

Ducky knocks on the bathroom door.

"Can't you come out now?" she asks.

Piggy looks up from his book.

"I told you,"

he says through the door.

"I am sitting on the potty."

Ducky wears a nappy.

It feels cold.

It feels wet.

Ducky wriggles out

of her nappy.

She kicks her nappy

across the floor.

Knock, knock, knock!

"Let me in," says Ducky.

"I have to use the potty."

"You wear nappies!" says Piggy.

"Not any more," says Ducky.

"No more nappies for Ducky!"

Piggy pulls up his pants.

He washes his hands.

He opens the door.

He lets Ducky into the bathroom.

Now Piggy plays with his toys.

He reads his books.

After a while, he calls,

"Come out and play, Ducky."

"I can't play now," says Ducky.

"I am sitting on the potty!"